About the Author

GEORGE ELIOT
1819 – 1880

Silas Marner was published in 1861 at a time when it was not acceptable for woman to write novels. Mary Ann Evans, the author, chose the pen name George Eliot to hide the fact that she was not a man.

George Eliot told several stories about good overcoming evil so some people thought she might be a clergyman. Other people thought she might be a clergyman's wife, but no one ever guessed her true identity.

In the story of *Silas Marner*, George Eliot describes how Eppie finds Silas and he takes care of her. Eppie was lucky to find him because many children in the same situation would have been taken to the workhouse. There, they would have worked long hours to earn their keep. The fortunate ones might have been taken as apprentices and taught a trade. The unfortunate ones would have to work as kitchen maids and farm labourers for the rest of their lives.

TREETOPS CLASSICS

Silas Marner

GEORGE ELIOT
adapted by Shirley Isherwood

OXFORD
UNIVERSITY PRESS

OXFORD

UNIVERSITY PRESS

Great Clarendon Street, Oxford OX2 6DP

Oxford University Press is a department of the University of Oxford.
It furthers the University's objective of excellence in research, scholarship,
and education by publishing worldwide in

Oxford New York

Athens Auckland Bangkok Bogotá Buenos Aires Cape Town
Chennai Dar es Salaam Delhi Florence Hong Kong Istanbul Karachi
Kolkata Kuala Lumpur Madrid Melbourne Mexico City Mumbai Nairobi
Paris São Paulo Shanghai Singapore Taipei Tokyo Toronto Warsaw

with associated companies in Berlin Ibadan

Oxford is a registered trade mark of Oxford University Press
in the UK and in certain other countries

British Library Cataloguing in Publication Data

Data available

ISBN 0 19 919442 4

Cover illustration: Paul Hunt
Inside illustrations: Chris Molam

Printed by Ebenezer Baylis and Son Ltd, Worcester

www.oup.com/uk/primary

CONTENTS

PART ONE

CHAPTER I

Silas the Stranger

A linen-weaver called Silas Marner lived alone in a small stone cottage. It stood all but hidden amongst the hedgerows that grew thick round the village of Raveloe. Nuts grew in the hedges in autumn and children trooped along the lanes to gather them. They called to one another as they worked, their voices full of laughter. But as twilight fell, and the baskets grew heavy, the children became tired and hungry and fell silent.

Then the sound of the linen-weaver's loom could be heard: a steady Clack! Clack! Clack! It came with such a regular beat that it was hard to imagine that it was being made by a human being.

Now, hearing the sound of the loom in the quiet dusk, the children hurried on, clutching their baskets and basins. As they went, they repeated to one another the stories they had heard about the weaver.

'If you're ill, he can cure you with herbs. Herbs that only *he* knows about.'

'Herbs grown in the Devil's garden, my mother says!'

'If he stares into your eyes he can cast a spell on you!'

'Sometimes the Devil takes his soul, my grandma

says! He takes his soul, and Silas has to stand like a statue until the Devil gives it back!'

They were nearing the village now; lights could be seen in the cottage windows. The sight made the children bolder, and the most frightening tale of all was now told. 'Sometimes he dies, then comes back to life! Jem Rodney saw it with his own eyes!'

With that they scattered and went their separate ways.

But two of the tales told of Silas were true. He *could* cure many illnesses by the use of herbs, and he *had* been seen to stand as still and staring as a dead man. The mole-catcher, Jem, told the story many times in the Rainbow Inn. Each time he told it, his listeners crowded round. And each time his listeners added their own explanation of this awful sight.

'It was evening, and I was on my way homeward,' said Jem, 'when, all of a sudden, I see him standing in the lane, with a heavy bag on his back. Now any man who still had his senses would have set the bag down on the ground.'

'True, true,' came the murmured agreement of his listeners.

'But not he,' said Jem, 'and when I come up to him I see his eyes were like glass. I spoke to him, and he made no reply. I shook him and his limbs were stiff, and his hands clutched at his bag like hands made of iron. I'd just about made up my mind that he was dead, when he came all right again, said, "Good night," to me and walked off.'

'Well, it's my belief,' said one of the listeners, 'that he had a fit.'

'Never! Never,' said Mr Macey, who was clerk of the parish, and as such was respected as a clever and learned man. ''As anyone ever been known to go off into a fit, and not fall down?'

'But there is such a thing as a man's soul being let loose from his body,' said another eager listener. 'It goes out like a bird from its nest, and that's how such folk gets to know what they know. They flies unseen and hears things, learns things.'

Heads nodded at this. This was a very likely explanation of why Silas never paid a visit to the inn, never needed company, never seemed in fact to stop working at his loom, except for the times when he delivered his bolts of cloth to his customers and collected his yarn.

'And what does he do with the money he earns from all that work?' someone asked. 'He must have a good lot of gold hidden away!'

Heads nodded more vigorously at this. Then the talk turned to other subjects.

But again, as with the talk of the children, two of the things said about Silas were true; the fact that he suffered from fits, and the statement that he had gold hidden away in his cottage.

CHAPTER 2

The Crime in Lantern Yard

Silas had lived so long in his hidden cottage that no one now wondered what his life had been before he came to Raveloe. But they would have been astonished to learn that in those far off days, in the time he spent in Lantern Yard, his life had been full. He had companions, one close friend in particular, William Dane, and he was engaged to a pretty serving girl, Sarah.

He attended chapel without fail each week, and it was during the service one Sunday that he had fallen down in a fit. He lay unconscious for over an hour, while the chapel members crowded round him and spoke in whispers.

'He is in a trance,' said the minister. 'He is marked by God as being someone special.' The members of the chapel knew that Silas suffered from fits, but this was the first they had witnessed.

'This seems to me to be more of the work of Satan, than that of our Lord!' said Silas's friend, William Dane.

If any member of the chapel thought it strange that William should speak so of his friend they said nothing. William was a very religious young man, and when he came to realize that he was jealous of his friend, then he would banish the feeling from his heart, of this they were sure. After all, they said, it was only human nature to sometimes feel envious of even a dear friend. And Sarah was, they murmured amongst themselves, a very pretty girl.

But William did not banish the feeling of jealousy; instead the feeling grew. In the disguise of friendly concern, he asked Silas if he did not hold some black thing in his soul.

Disturbed by this, Silas turned to Sarah, but she seemed to draw away from him, as if she too thought he held some dark and evil secret.

It was at this time that an elder of the chapel fell ill. He was an old man without family, and Silas and William took turns to sit by his bed. One night Silas became suddenly aware that the old man's breathing had stopped. It was as if he had drawn an easy breath one moment and, in the next instant, stopped.

Leaning over the bed, and touching the elder's face and hands, he found them to be cold as iron. He knew then that the old man had been dead for some time.

'Have I been asleep?' Silas wondered, puzzled and disturbed by his discovery. He glanced at the clock and saw that it was four in the morning. 'And where is William?' he thought. 'It was his turn to take over the watch some hours ago. Has he fallen ill, too?'

In a state of agitation, Silas went to seek help from the minister of the chapel. The minister assured him that he would go at once to the elder's house, and that he would also make enquiries about William. At this, Silas hurried to his work, confident that the minister would do all that he said he would.

He was greatly surprised and alarmed when, at six in the evening, both the minister and William appeared and told him that he was to go at once to the chapel to meet the chapel members there.

Neither William nor the minister said anything further, until Silas was seated in the chapel before the members, whose eyes fixed on him solemnly.

Then the minister took a knife from his pocket and showed it to Silas.

'Do you know where you left this knife?' he asked.

Silas, who recognized the knife as his own, said that he did not know that he had left it anywhere other than in his pocket.

The minister stared hard at him, and the members of the chapel set up a low murmuring amongst themselves. What did this mean? Silas wondered, and felt his hands begin to tremble.

'In your pocket?' asked the minister. Silas nodded.

'Do not try to hide your sin!' the minister shouted at this. 'Confess! Repent! This knife was found on the chest by the elder's bed.'

'No . . .' said Silas, shaking his head.

'In the place where the bag that held church money was kept,' went on the minister. 'Some hand had removed that bag, and whose hand but the owner of this knife?'

The murmuring of the chapel members grew louder. Silas stood for a moment, mute with astonishment. Then, 'God will clear me!' he said in a loud clear voice. 'I know nothing of where the knife was found, nor of the money. Search my lodgings! You will find only three pounds of my own savings. William Dane knows that I have had those these last six months.'

'The proof is heavy against you, brother Silas,' said the minister. 'The money was taken last night, and there was no one at the elder's house but you. William Dane declares that he was kept away by a sudden sickness from taking his place there. You yourself said that he did not come. And you neglected the poor elder! The man was long dead, when I saw him. What were you doing?'

'I must have slept,' said Silas, 'or I might have fallen into a trance, such as you have seen before. But I say again, search me and my dwelling place, for I have been nowhere else!'

So the search was made. It ended with William Dane finding the empty bag that once held the church money, tucked behind a chest in Silas's room.

'Oh, Silas, confess!' cried William, holding the bag, and gazing beseechingly at his friend. 'Do not hide your sin any longer!'

'William,' said Silas, his own gaze on his friend was one of deep sorrow. 'We have been friends for nine years. Have you ever known me tell a lie? God will clear me!'

Then, his eyes still fixed on the face of his friend, a deep flush rose to his cheeks. He seemed about to say something, but checked himself.

'Yes, Silas?' asked the minister. 'Speak!'

The blood drained from Silas's cheeks, and he spoke in a low voice. 'I remember now – the knife was not in my pocket.'

William became uneasy under Silas's steady gaze. 'I don't know what he's talking about!' he exclaimed.

'Then where was it?' asked the minister.

'I cannot say,' said Silas, 'but God will clear me.' But he remembered quite clearly what he had done with his knife. He had used it to cut a leather band for William.

On the return to the chapel, the elders gathered together to hear what had happened and to decide if they found Silas innocent or guilty.

They found him guilty.

'You are no longer a member of this chapel, Silas Marner,' said the minister. 'Unless you confess, and give back the money, you will be treated as an outcast amongst us.'

Silas turned his gaze back upon his friend. 'The last time I remember using that knife was to cut a strap for you, William. I don't remember putting it back in my pocket. You stole the money, and have woven a plot to lay the blame on me. But you'll suffer for your sin! I have found today that there is no just, fair God!'

The elders gasped in horror at this. Silas Marner, the thief, was calling God a liar, and in God's own house.

He was indeed in the hands of the Devil!

Silas went home, and for a whole day sat alone, silent and stunned. The next day he comforted himself by working long and hard at his loom. In the evening, the minister and one of the elders came to deliver a message from Sarah that she no longer wished to marry him.

Silas said nothing to this, but just turned back to his work. Soon after, he left Lantern Yard, never to return.

CHAPTER 3

The Gold

When Silas came to Raveloe it was as if he had journeyed to a foreign land. No cottages stood near to his own, and the land surrounding was a wilderness of bushes and narrow lanes. Close by, was the quarry known as the Stone-pits. Silas heard the explosions that were made as the stone was quarried. On his solitary walks he noted the deep hollows that had been left after the stone had been taken – he saw too how quickly they filled with rain, making great, still lakes. It was, he thought, a fearsome place.

At first he hoped that his faith in God and in his fellow man would return, but as time went on he felt as numb as on the day when the elders had found him guilty of theft, and he had discovered William's treachery.

Once more, he threw himself into his work for comfort. The steady sound of the loom shut out all thought, and he began to work far into the night. In this way he finished an order for table linen much earlier than was expected. Five bright golden guineas were put into his hand for this work, much to his great surprise. He had never been paid so highly before, having always worked for a merchant, who had given him a much lower rate of pay, and who then sold the work on at a profit. Silas had given most of his pay away in acts of charity.

Now, making his way home over the fields, the thought came to him that the money clutched in his palm was his alone, for he was no longer part of a group whose members sometimes needed help. The thought was consoling, and as soon as he reached his cottage, he tucked the coins away behind a loose brick.

Once more at his loom, a picture of them gleaming in the palm of his hand came to him as he worked. If he could not be welcomed and respected by his fellow man, if even God it seemed had turned away from him, then at least he had his gold.

Soon after this, there arose a chance for Silas to become part of the lives of those around him. One day, when taking a pair of shoes to be mended, he saw the cobbler's wife, Sally, huddled by the fire, gasping for breath. Silas knew what the trouble was; he knew also which herbs would help her.

When Sally recovered, word went swiftly round that Silas was not only a weaver of good linen, but also a wise man – a man, it was whispered, who could cure illness by charms. Silas suddenly found mothers with their children on his doorstep, begging him to charm away sickness, whooping cough, measles, fevers. Farm workers came to him for help with injuries, old people with aches and pains. All wanted a charm, something they could put in a pocket, or hang round a child's neck in a little bag.

There had been a wise woman in the village long ago who gave charms and muttered spells. Surely Silas, who had cured a dying woman, was one such as she had been? They offered him silver, which he refused; the herbs were put there by God, he said, and were free for all to use. And they didn't believe him when he told them that charms did not cure. In their ignorance they wanted magic as well as medicine. With Silas's refusal to give them magic they turned away from him.

Once more Silas went back to his loom. The years passed, the pile of gold, hidden behind the loose brick, grew. At night Silas put the shutters up against his windows, barred his doors and poured the gold out on table. He counted it, set it in little columns, or just sat gazing at it gleaming in the light of his fire. It was the one bright thing in his life.

Then, just before Christmas, fifteen years after he had come to Raveloe, something happened which changed his life for ever.

CHAPTER 4

Godfrey and Dunsey

The most important, and the richest man in Raveloe was Squire Cass, who lived in the Red House with his two sons. Their mother had died when the boys were very young, and the squire brought them up as well as he knew how. But many thought that he would have done better to have hired a good nanny, or better still, to have married again.

Godfrey and his younger brother Dunstan ran wild as children. As grown young men they did little, neither worked nor took an interest in their father's estate. It seemed enough that the land brought in money for them to live in the way that they liked. In Dunstan's case this was to spend his days gambling and drinking.

Dunstan, commonly known as Dunsey, was not well liked in the village. He was spiteful, and thought of no one but himself.

His brother Godfrey had a much nicer nature, but even he, it was whispered, was beginning to show signs of behaving in the same way as his young brother. Sometimes he disappeared for days, although no one knew where he went.

'It will be a thousand pities if he starts to behave like Dunsey,' said the gossips, shaking their heads.

'He will lose Nancy Lammeter, that's for sure! And what a wonderful mistress of the Red House she would make!' said the wagging tongues. 'It would be the making of them all, Squire included! It's well known that the Lammeters are all brought up to waste not as much as a pinch of salt.'

'But for all that, they're not mean – just careful, wise.'

The tongues wagged more sharply, and the heads shook more solemnly when it was seen that Godfrey began to look pale and ill.

◆◆◆

One November afternoon, Godfrey sat waiting for Dunsey. He was alone, save for his dog, Snuff, and he seemed uneasy. As soon as Dunsey entered the room, Godfrey spoke.

'Father thinks that Fowler the farmer hasn't paid the rent he owes for the land. He's told me that he'll throw Fowler out if he doesn't pay.'

'What's that to me?' muttered Dunsey.

'You know full well,' said Godfrey. 'Fowler gave the rent money to me a month ago. It was the hundred pounds that I gave to you!'

Dunsey laughed. 'Well, you were kind enough to give

it to me, you can be even kinder and pay it back!'

Godfrey clenched his fists and half rose from his chair. 'I'll beat it out of you!' he exclaimed.

'Oh no, you won't,' said his brother. 'I can have you turned out of this house, cut off without a shilling, if I told father how you are secretly married to Molly Farren!'

'Hold your tongue!' cried Godfrey.

Dunsey just grinned and went on.

'If I told father that this Molly is a drunk, if I told him that you couldn't bear the sight of her any more, you'd never see a penny of his money. He'd disown you, and everything would come to me.'

What Dunsey said was true; Godfrey knew this. He was in his brother's power.

'Where can I get a hundred pounds?' he said despairingly. 'I haven't a shilling to my name.'

'Sell your horse,' said Dunsey. 'Sell Wildfire.'

'But I need the money *now!*' said Godfrey.

'Ride him at the hunt tomorrow,' said Dunsey. 'Bryce will be there. He told me last week that he's looking for a good horse.'

'I can't go to the hunt,' replied Godfrey. 'I'm going to Mrs Osgood's birthday party.'

Dunsey grinned. 'And will the lovely Miss Nancy Lammeter be there?'

'That's enough!' said Godfrey shortly.

'You can't marry the lovely Nancy, can you? But take heart, brother. Perhaps Molly will drink herself to death. *Then* you would be free to do so – unless someone told Nancy our little secret.'

Godfrey rose and grabbed his brother by the arm. 'I'll tell *you* something, brother! My patience is almost at an end. I have been thinking of going to Father and telling him all. If I did, I should get *you* off my back if nothing else.'

Dunsey pulled at his sleeve but couldn't loosen Godfrey's grip, and he saw from his brother's face that he meant to have his say.

'If you go on like this,' said Godfrey, 'I may as well tell Father everything! You drain me of money, so I've nothing left to give to *her* for her drink and drugs. And if I don't give her money, then she threatens to come here and tell him herself!'

He loosened his grip, and Dunsey let his arm fall limply at his side. He knew that he had gone too far. 'Do as you please,' he said, as lightly as he could. He sat down and gazed at his brother, who stood by the fire. He was big and powerful, and no coward; but Dunsey knew that he would never carry out his threat to tell his father the whole story. He would have to sell his beloved horse.

'Let me sell Wildfire for you,' he said. 'Let me ride him to the hunt.'

'What! Trust my horse to *you!*' cried Godfrey.

'You have no choice, brother,' said Dunsey. 'Let me sell him. I'll do it fair and square. I'll get a hundred and twenty pounds for him.'

He rose and made his way to the door. 'You've got the family looks, brother, but I have the luck!'

With that he grinned and left, slamming the door behind him.

The next day Dunsey set off for the hunt, riding Wildfire. He carried a gold-handled whip, and carried it in such a way as anyone whom he met would see it and be impressed. Dunsey was a vain man, and jealous of anything that had to do with his brother: his looks, his nature, or his possessions. It was a raw, cold day and as he passed by the weaver's cottage and heard the clack of the loom, the thought came to him that perhaps Silas would lend his brother the money. 'The old fool is said to have a fortune hidden away,' he told himself, slowing Wildfire to a walk. 'If we could persuade, or frighten him into lending the money, then there would be no need for Godfrey to sell his horse.'

And then he smiled. What better way of hurting his brother than to force him to part with his beloved Wildfire! With this thought he urged the animal into a trot and rode on.

He met up with Bryce at the hunt. 'He's mine now!' he said, patting Wildfire's neck. 'Godfrey got tired of him, but I don't want to keep him. Are you interested?'

'Indeed I am,' said Bryce. 'How much?'

'A hundred and twenty pounds,' said Dunsey.

'The money will be paid when the horse is in my stables, safe and sound,' said Bryce.

'Agreed!' said Dunsey, leaning from the saddle to shake hands.

Had Dunsey been wise he would have ridden the horse to Bryce's stables straight away. But he was a proud man, and wanted to show off his horsemanship, and Wildfire was just the animal to help him do this.

But the ground that day was wet and slippery. The horse fell on taking a high fence, and a fence-post pierced his heart. He died at once.

Dunsey was thrown from the saddle, unhurt. He stood gazing down at the beautiful animal that had, only a moment ago, been alive and strong. The thought crossed his mind, 'How will I tell Godfrey?' Then he dismissed it with a shrug of his shoulders. The sorrows of others did not affect Dunsey for very long.

When he regained his breath, he set out to walk home across the fields. A mist had arisen, for which he was thankful; being a proud man he did not wish to be seen making his way on foot. As he went, the mist thickened so that he could hardly see before him and had to feel his way along the lanes by touching the hedgerows with his whip. The whip was Godfrey's and had a gold handle with Godfrey's initials. Dunsey had taken it without asking permission, as he usually did with the possessions of others.

After he had gone some distance in this manner he saw the light from the weaver's cottage gleaming dimly through the fog. This made Dunsey think once more about the gold that the old man was said to have saved.

'And saved over fifteen years,' Dunsey told himself. 'He must have quite a hoard by now.'

He reached the cottage door and knocked loudly. There was no reply, and after a moment Dunsey raised the latch and gave a gentle push. To his surprise the door swung open, and he peered in to see a bright fire, three chairs and a table. There was no sign of Silas Marner.

Dunsey sat by the fire to dry his wet clothes. 'Where was the old man?' he wondered. 'What could take him out on such a night?' He could not have been long gone, for the fire was well banked up, and a piece of meat hung from a skewer.

'His supper,' Dunsey told himself, with a spiteful smile. 'The old miser doesn't live on dry bread as everyone thinks.'

But what was keeping Silas out in the damp, misty night? Had he perhaps gone for firewood, and slipped and cracked open his skull?

'And if he has,' pondered Dunsey, gazing into the flames, 'who would his money belong to? Who would

know where it was hidden? Who would know if
someone took it away?'

He rose to his feet and looked round the room. There
were only three places where he had heard of cottagers
hiding their gold – the thatch, the bed, or a hole in the
floor. The weaver's cottage had no thatch, and Dunsey
was making his way to the bed when his eye fell on the
floor. The sand that covered it was evenly spread, except
for where the loom stood. There, it was laid more thickly,
and had the imprint of fingers.

Dunsey crouched, swept away the sand with his whip, then pushed the end between the bricks and saw that they were loose. Working with speed, he lifted two of the bricks. Two bags lay beneath.

'The money!' he muttered, lifting them and feeling their weight. 'And a good deal of it, too!'

He thought no further then, but replaced the bricks and swept the sand over to cover them. Then he left the cottage carrying the bags, closing the door behind him so that darkness lay all round and hid him from sight.

CHAPTER 5

The Theft

When Dunsey left the cottage, Silas Marner was not more than a hundred yards away, plodding through the mist and rain with a sack over his head and shoulders and a lantern in his hand. As Dunsey had supposed, he had been down the lane to get wood for his fire.

Supper was his favourite meal, and he looked forward especially to this one for it had cost him nothing. Miss Priscilla Lammeter had given it to him, as well as his fee, for she had been delighted with the linen that he had woven for her. So it was with a great feeling of satisfaction that he pushed open his door and entered his cottage.

At first nothing seemed changed to his short-sighted eyes. He sat by his fire, and examined the piece of meat. It was not yet fully cooked and he sighed a little with impatience. It was his habit after supper to lay his gold out on the table. But on this evening, he decided not to wait for the pleasure of seeing his gold but rose, placed his candle on the floor by the loom, and swept away the sand. Then he lifted the two bricks, saw the empty space beneath, and his heart leapt in his chest.

At first he could not believe what he saw, and reached a trembling hand into the hole and felt about it. Still not wanting to accept that his gold had gone, he rose and began to search the room, telling himself that for some reason he had put it away in a new place and that he had forgotten where. ·

He searched every corner of his cottage, upturned his bed, and looked in the oven where he kept his firewood to dry. When there were no other places to search, he knelt once more and felt round the hole in the floor once more. Only then did he acknowledge the truth, and putting his hands to his head he gave a wild cry. Throwing open his door, he rushed out into the hard, driving rain.

The talk in the Rainbow Inn was as it was on most nights. The customers repeated old tales about the inhabitants of Raveloe – tales of whom had arrived when, and from where; of whom had prospered due to wisdom and hard work, whom had failed due to drink, or worse.

A favourite tale was told, that of haunted stables, where some said that they had truly seen a ghost, and some said that they had heard strange noises. Some said that they had seen neither ghost nor heard noises, but

had felt a presence so strong that they felt rooted to the spot with fear.

It was during this talk of ghosts, noises, and an unseen presence, that the door of the inn burst open and the thin pale figure of Silas staggered into the lamplight. He was as startling a sight as if he himself had come as a spirit from another world. The speakers fell silent, drew in their breath and held it for a moment.

The landlord was the first to gather his wits and approached the distraught figure.

'Master Marner!' he said. 'What has happened?'

'Robbed!' gasped Silas. 'I've been robbed. I want the constable – the magistrate – Squire Cass!' He looked round the room, his eyes wild. His glance fell on Jem Rodney, the poacher.

It was Jem! thought Silas. Who else but a poacher would have been out on such a wild night?

'*You!*' he cried, going towards the man. '*You* stole my money.'

He was stopped by the landlord who seized him by the arm and sat him down. 'Calm yourself Master Marner. Jem hasn't taken your money – he's been sitting here with the rest of us for most of the evening. Be calm and tell us what has happened.'

Silas told his story as best he could. His words came in little rushes and he was so distressed that all who heard him could not but believe him. But, they asked, turning one to another, who could have taken the money? Who

knew where it had been hidden? Who would know that
Silas was to leave his cottage at the time he did?

As they spoke amongst themselves, Silas's gaze
returned to Jem, and he recalled most clearly how he
himself had felt when he had been wrongly accused of
theft.

'I am sorry, Jem,' he said. 'I ought not to have said
what I did. You didn't take my money, I know that.'

'But somebody took it,' said old Mr Macey. 'That's
clear enough.'

'How much money has been stolen, Master Marner?'

asked Dowlas, the blacksmith.

'Two hundred and seventy pounds, twelve shillings, and sixpence,' said Silas with a groan.

'Not too heavy to carry,' said Dowlas. 'I tell you what I think, Silas. Some tramp chanced by, saw you leave the cottage, and took the opportunity to rob you.'

'But nothing in my house had been disturbed!' said Silas. 'Nothing! I had no suspicions until I looked in the place and found the money gone.'

'Now Silas,' said the landlord. 'Your eyes aren't good, we all know that. You know it, too. I suggest that two of us go with you to your cottage and see if we can't spot something that might lead us to the thief.'

Silas agreed that this was the best thing to do. With some rough sacks over his shoulders to protect him, he followed his companions out into the heavy rain, thinking of the long night hours to come.

CHAPTER 6

Godfrey Confesses

When Godfrey Cass returned from Mrs Osgood's party at midnight, he was surprised to find that his brother was not at home. Perhaps he had been unable to sell Wildfire, and was waiting for another chance. Or perhaps, it being a foggy night, he had decided to stay at the inn in Batherly.

'He could have sent word,' thought Godfrey, 'but what does he care about my suspense? What does Dunsey care about anyone save himself?'

The next morning he was caught up in the general excitement about the robbery. He, like everyone else, was busy gathering and discussing news about it and, for the time being, all thoughts of his brother and Wildfire vanished from his mind.

A tinderbox had been found, and the general opinion was that it belonged to a tinker who had passed through Raveloe last month. Almost at once it was decided that he must have been the thief. Why?

'He wore earrings,' said Mr Snell, the landlord of the Rainbow Inn. 'He had black curly hair, and he had a *look*.'

'What sort of a look?' he was asked.

'A *look*,' said Snell, 'that made me feel uneasy. There's no telling why – it just did.'

Well, someone who wore earrings and was capable of giving looks that caused unease would most likely also be a thief; that too was agreed upon. Heads nodded wisely, and Godfrey, both amused and disgusted by this line of reasoning, lost interest in the robbery. His thoughts returned to Wildfire and Dunsey, and he mounted a horse and rode off down the lane in search of them.

He had not gone far when he saw Mr Bryce riding towards him.

'Well, Mr Godfrey, what a lucky brother of yours he is, that Master Dunsey!' said Bryce.

'What do you mean?' asked Godfrey, hastily.

' Why, hasn't he been home yet?' asked Bryce.

'No,' said Godfrey. 'What has happened? What has he done with my horse?'

'Ah!' said Bryce, 'I thought that it was yours! He pretended that you'd given it to him.'

'Has he brought it down and broken its knees?' exclaimed Godfrey.

'Worse that that,' said Bryce. 'I'd made a bargain to buy it from him for a hundred and twenty pounds – a high price, but I have always liked the animal. But what does Dunsey do but fly at a hedge with stakes in it! The poor creature was pierced through the heart, and had been dead a good while before it was found.'

'And my brother?' asked Godfrey.

'Alive and well, as far as I know,' said Bryce. 'Although no one has seen him. But never fear, he hasn't been hurt.'

'Hurt?' said Godfrey, bitterly. 'He'll never be hurt – he's made to hurt others.'

He turned his horse and began to ride back to the Red House. There was only one course open to him now, he thought – he must tell his father everything.

'I shall tell him that I was forced to give the money to

Dunsey,' he told himself. Then he realized that if he did this, Dunsey, out of spite and a wish for revenge, would tell their father about Godfrey's secret marriage.

'Perhaps there *is* a way to keep him silent,' pondered Godfrey. 'I could tell father that I took the money Fowler gave me. Father will be furious with me. But I've never done such a thing before, and the storm will pass – he'll forgive me.'

But the nearer he drew to home, the more clearly it came to him that he could not tell this lie. 'I don't pretend to be a saint,' he told himself, 'but I'm no scoundrel! I shall just tell him about *my* part in all this, and no more. I would never have kept the money for myself. Dunsey blackmailed me, and that's the truth.'

The next morning, when Squire Cass was having breakfast, Godfrey came into the room. 'Father,' he said, 'I must speak to you. It's about Wildfire . . .'

'Broken a leg has he?' asked the Squire. 'I thought you a better rider than that! I never brought a horse down in my life. And if I had I could have whistled for a mount, for my father would never have given me another horse. You boys have been spoiled.'

'Father,' said Godfrey, 'Wildfire's been killed. But I wasn't going to ask you to buy me another horse.

Dunsey took him to the hunt yesterday, to sell him for me, and after he'd made a bargain with Bryce, he rode him and killed him. If it hadn't been for that, I should have paid you a hundred pounds this morning.'

The Squire frowned at this. 'You don't owe me a hundred pounds,' he said.

'The truth is, sir,' said Godfrey, 'I'm sorry, but Fowler paid me the hundred pounds which he owed you when I was over there last month. Dunsey bothered me for the money and I gave it to him, hoping that I would be able to pay you back before this.'

The Squire had grown red with rage long before his son had finished speaking, and now found it difficult to speak.

'*You let Dunsey have it!*' he brought out at last. 'And how long have you been so thick with your brother that you plot with him to cheat me out of my money?'

He paused, choked by anger. Godfrey stood silent.

'Let Dunsey have the money!' the Squire said again. 'Why should you let Dunsey have the money? There's some lie at the bottom of this!'

'No lie,' said Godfrey. 'I meant to pay it back and that's the whole story. I never meant to cheat you. You've never known me do a dishonest trick, sir.'

'Where's Dunsey then?' asked his father, growing somewhat calmer. 'Let him give me an account of what he needed the money for. Go on! Fetch him.'

'Dunsey's not back, sir,' said Godfrey.

'What? Did he break his neck in the hunt?'

'No, he's unhurt, but I don't know where he is,' said Godfrey.

'You don't know, eh?' said his father, obviously not believing him. 'I know what it is. You've been up to some trick and are bribing him not to tell. Am I right, sir?'

Godfrey was startled by how close to the truth his father had come.

'No, sir,' he said, trying to speak lightly. 'It's just a young man's foolishness, nothing more.'

'Foolishness – rubbish!' returned his father. 'It's high time you settled down. And I tell you, you won't find a better bride than Lammeter's daughter.' He looked keenly at his son. 'You like the lass well enough, don't you?'

Godfrey nodded.

'Has she refused you then?' the Squire asked.

'I haven't asked her to marry me,' muttered Godfrey.

'Then do so,' said his father, 'or, if you have not the courage, let me say a word to her father.'

'I'd rather let things be,' said Godfrey, 'and I hope you won't try to hurry it on by saying anything.' He felt uneasy, for the interview had taken a turn that he had not expected.

'I shall do as I like,' said the Squire. 'I am master here! Now go and tell Winthrop to saddle my horse. I shall speak with Fowler this morning. And tell Winthrop to sell Dunsey's horse, and hand the money over to *me*. He'll keep no more horses at *my* expense. And if you see your brother, sir, tell him from me not to bother coming back home. I never want to see him again!'

'I will tell him what you say, sir,' replied Godfrey. He felt a great sense of relief at having confessed to his father about the hundred pounds that he had given to

Dunsey. He felt even more relieved when his father did not press the matter as to why he had passed the money over to his brother. 'If I can only manage to keep my marriage to Molly a secret,' he told himself, 'then all will be well. But if Father finds out, if Dunsey tells him after all . . .'. He couldn't bear to think any more on the subject and forced his mind on to other matters.

CHAPTER 7

Christmas at Raveloe

Time passed, and the excitement about the robbery died down. Justice Malam, who was highly regarded in Raveloe, began an inquiry concerning the tinderbox and the peddler, name unknown, who had black curly hair and who wore an earring. But as this description could be applied to almost every peddler who passed through the village, the inquiry revealed nothing at all.

The absence of Dunsey Cass was scarcely noticed. He had quarrelled with his father before, and had stayed away for six weeks. No one thought to connect him with the robbery.

But even though the excitement about the robbery had died, there was still much talk about it, and now the speakers were divided into two camps. One group favoured the tinderbox-peddler theory, while the other group insisted that the money had been spirited away by some magical means.

While this talk gave the customers of the inn entertainment and amusement, poor Silas lived in a state of blank unhappiness. His thoughts, which had for so long settled on the two main things in his life, his work and his gold, now found themselves like birds whose nests have been destroyed; they fluttered about with no comforting place in which to settle.

At least one good thing came from the robbery; the villagers now saw Silas in a more kindly light. They began to greet him when they met him in the streets; some brought him food. Even the vicar, whose opinion was that Silas had lost his gold because he thought too much of it, and never came to church, brought him a pair of pig's trotters.

People began to call on him. One evening, so close to Christmas that the scents of Christmas cooking were in the air, Mr Macey, the old town clerk paid him a visit. 'Come Master Marner,' he said, 'you mustn't sit alone like this. You must keep up your spirits.'

But Silas, so long used to being an outcast, could no longer respond to a friendly gesture. He sat still at his loom, his head in his hands.

Mr Macey tried once more.

'A suit, now Master Marner,' he said. 'Do you have a Sunday suit?'

Silas shook his head.

'Well now, I advise you to get one,' said Mr Macey. 'Why, with a good suit on your back you would be able to come to church of a Sunday and mix with us all a bit more!'

Silas roused himself with an effort. 'Thank you,' he said, 'I will.' He said no more and after a while, when Mr Macey himself could think of nothing further to say, the visit came to an end.

On a Sunday, soon after this, Silas was visited by Dolly Winthrop. She brought with her some lardy cakes and her seven-year-old son, Aaron. As the two made their way up the lane, they heard the sound of the loom. 'Just as I thought,' said Dolly.

'You were working,' she said, when Silas opened the door.

'I work every day,' said Silas.

He took the cakes that she held out to him, and

thanked her, and gestured towards a chair. Dolly sat, with Aaron clinging close by her side and gazing at Silas with a clear steady gaze. He was rather afraid of the weaver.

'But today's the Lord's day,' said Dolly. 'Didn't you ever go to church at the place where you lived before?'

'No, never,' said Silas. 'I went to chapel.'

Dolly was puzzled by this word, chapel, which was new to her, but thought it best not to ask what it meant in case it was the name for some haunts of sin and wickedness.

'Well, Master Marner,' she said, 'turn over a new leaf. Come to church. You've no idea how much better the words of our minister can make you feel, or how the praying and the singing can lift your heart.'

Silas stared at her, and she brought Aaron forwards from behind her chair where he had crouched.

'Sing for the gentleman,' she said, then turned back to Silas.

'He has the voice of a little bird,' she said proudly.

Aaron remained silent and, to encourage him, Silas held out the plate of cakes. Aaron at once took a cake, but still did not sing. He continued to stare mutely at Silas, while slowly raising the cake to his mouth.

His mother took it from him. 'That's naughty!' she said. 'Sing, and then you shall have it.'

So Aaron sang.

'God rest you, merry gentlemen,

Let nothing you dismay,

For Jesus Christ our Saviour

Was born on Christmas day.'

'There!' said Dolly, when the carol was ended. 'Doesn't he sing pretty, Master Marner?'

'Yes, very,' said Silas. The effect of the music upon him was not, he knew, what Dolly had hoped. Far from raising his spirits, it deepened his sadness. But she means well, he told himself, and was kind, and the only way that occurred to him to show his gratitude was to offer Aaron more cake.

'No, no,' said Dolly, rising and taking her son's hand. 'He's had enough, thank you kindly. We must be leaving. But Master Marner, if you need anything, someone to clean or cook a little food for you, you have only to ask.'

They left and Silas sat once more at his loom. It was, he felt, as though all the love and affection and trust he had once had for his fellow man was still there, but somehow locked away like a treasure which he could no longer enjoy. The next day was Christmas day, and he spent it alone.

The big party given at the Red House by the Squire was not on Christmas day, but on New Year's Eve. The best society in Raveloe was invited and all the prettiest girls. Some guests came long distances to attend. Spare bedrooms were made ready for them, and the house stocked with enough food as though it was preparing for a siege.

Dunsey had still not returned, but at the family party on Christmas day no one had remarked on his absence. Godfrey, while looking forward to the New Year, told himself that his brother would surely return in time for the party.

'Then he might tell father all about your marriage to Molly,' said an anxious voice in his mind.

'No, no,' said Godfrey, trying to reassure himself. 'On second thoughts, he won't come, and I shall sit by Nancy and get a kind look from her.'

'But you need money,' persisted the anxious voice. 'You need money for Molly. When Dunsey returns, he is sure to ask you for more. How will you get it without selling something that you hold dear – your mother's diamond pin, say? And if you *don't* get it . . . what then?'

'Something may happen to make things easier,' Godfrey told himself. 'I won't spoil the pleasure of being with Nancy! I won't think of money or Dunsey or anything but Nancy's eyes looking into mine and the feel of her hand in mine!'

But the anxious voice went on, and neither the noisy Christmas company nor drink could quieten it.

CHAPTER 8

The Ball

Miss Nancy Lammeter made her way to the New Year's Eve party riding behind her father on his horse. The sky was dark and heavy with snow not yet fallen, but Nancy's cheeks glowed at the thought of the evening that lay ahead. Then, as they drew near to the Red House, she saw, to her dismay, that Godfrey Cass was waiting to lift her down. At this sight, she wished with all her heart that her sister Priscilla had been riding ahead, then Godfrey would be forced to help her instead.

'Have I not made it clear,' she asked herself, 'that I do not want to marry him, not if he asked me a hundred times or more! Anyway, I do not believe he means it when he asks,' she went on. 'Sometimes he does not even speak to me for weeks on end. And some say that he is going the same way as his brother, that no-good Dunsey. Oh, if only he wasn't standing there, waiting for me.'

Luck was on her side, for as they drew near to the house, the Squire and a whole merry crowd came down the steps to welcome them and Nancy felt herself lifted down by a pair of strong arms which belonged to a smiling stranger.

But as soon as the ball began, Godfrey hurried to her side. 'Will you dance with me, Miss Nancy?' he asked.

Good manners prevented Nancy from saying anything other than, 'Yes.' It was clear that she was not about to dance with anyone else. The word was said coldly, however.

She and Godfrey circled the floor together, catching the eye of many of the other guests. They made a handsome couple and were a pleasure to watch. Then suddenly the pair vanished from sight. 'Sweethearts!' was the thought in most heads. 'Lovers wanting to be alone!'

The truth was rather different. The foot of a dancer had caught in the hem of Nancy's dress and torn it. Flustered, she gathered up the skirt and stood, unsure of what to do. Godfrey, eager for a chance to help her, took her arm and led her into a small room nearby.

'Shall I find Priscilla and bring her to you?' he asked. But there was no need for him to do this, for at that very moment Priscilla, who had seen what happened to her sister, came hurrying to the room.

' I shall find needle and thread, and everything will be made right!' she exclaimed, and hurried out again.

'I'll wait with you,' said Godfrey, when Priscilla had gone; his offer was quickly rejected by Nancy.

'Thank you,' she said, 'I do not wish to give you any

more trouble. Go back to the dance. There are partners enough waiting for you.' She said this with a sideways glance at Godfrey, hoping in her heart that he would stay.

'Nancy,' said Godfrey, 'you know that I would rather dance with you than with any other woman in the world.'

'I know nothing of the sort,' said Nancy.

'Could you never like me then?' asked Godfrey. 'If you do not like me as I am, then I will change, be anything you wish, give up anything you do not like, be a better man in every way.'

'Good,' said Nancy, her voice still cool. 'I am glad to see a change for the better in anyone.'

At this point, Priscilla returned, carrying needle and thread. 'Now, let's look at this gown!' she said.

'I suppose that I had better go now,' said Godfrey.

'It's no matter to me whether you stay or go,' replied Nancy.

'Do you *want* me to go?' asked Godfrey.

'Do as you please,' replied Nancy.

'Then I'll stay,' said Godfrey.

While the guests danced at the Red House, and while Godfrey stood by Nancy's side, unwilling to leave her even for a second, his wife Molly was making her way along the lanes of Raveloe. She carried her child, Godfrey's daughter, in her arms. Snow had begun to fall heavily, and she pulled the worn shawl more tightly round the child to protect it.

She had planned this journey for a long while, brooding on how she would march into the Red House, and show the Squire the child that had Godfrey's hair and eyes. Then let Godfrey Cass deny that she was his wife!

There was a ball at the Red House every New Year's Eve, she knew that. The guests would be laughing, feasting. The women would be wearing beautiful silk and satin dresses. She, Molly, would burst in upon them, and stand before them in her rags. Then they would all, every one of them, turn on Godfrey Cass and no longer think him the gentleman! How could they think him to be a kind and honest man, seeing his wife in such a state?

But deep in her heart, Molly knew that her rags and faded looks were no fault of Godfrey's. The fault was her own, for she was addicted to opium. She was enslaved to it. It had driven out all sense of decency except for the feeling of tenderness that she still had for her child.

She had set out early on her journey, but when snow began to fall she told herself that she would do better to wait in whatever warm hut or barn was near. She had waited longer than she knew, and now found herself in the long, dark snow-bound lane which led to Raveloe.

Not knowing how close she was to the Red House, fear took hold of her. The picture of her entry into the ballroom no longer comforted her. Something of greater comfort lay tucked in the shawl with her child. Thrusting her hand amongst the folds, Molly drew out a small glass bottle, uncorked it, drank the contents, and threw the empty bottle away.

As she walked on, the snow ceased to fall, the clouds began to break, and through them an icy wind began to blow. Molly did not feel the cold; all she felt was a strong desire for sleep. She sank down at the side of the lane, and for a while held her child as closely as she had held her when she had been awake. Soon, her arms fell away, the shawl was loosened, and the child, feeling the cold wind, opened her eyes.

'Mammy!' she cried, trying to snuggle back into the warmth of her mother's body. But the arms would no longer hold her, and the child tumbled away from her mother, and down into the lane.

For a moment she stood, about to cry, then a bright light, which seemed to dance about on the white ground like some fairy thing, caught her eye. She began to make her way towards it, dragging the ragged shawl behind her, and with her little bonnet dangling at her back.

In this way, she toddled through the open door of Silas Marner's cottage.

CHAPTER 9

The Arrival of Eppie

But where was Silas when this little visitor came? He was in the cottage, asleep – fast asleep. That morning, Silas had been told by a neighbour to leave his cottage door open that night, so that he might hear the bells that rang in the new year.

'It brings good luck!' said his neighbour. 'It may even bring back your gold!'

Silas did not believe this. When twilight fell, he went often to his door and looked out. The snow was falling, and he closed the door each time before returning to his loom. But the last time he looked out, the snow no longer fell and the sky was growing clear.

Silas peered down the dark lane. He stood for a long time. There really was something on that road coming towards him, he felt it strongly! Then he was seized by a fit and knew nothing more. He stood holding his open door, powerless to stop whatever might enter – be it good or evil.

After the fit, Silas fell into a deep sleep. When he regained his senses, he huddled in his chair by the fire to get warm. Two logs had fallen apart and were sending out a red glimmer of light. Leaning forward to push them together, his blurred vision glanced on what seemed to be gold spread there before him on his hearth.

'My gold!' he thought. 'My gold has come back to me!' His heart beat wildly, and he stretched out his hand. Instead of the hard coins that he expected to feel, his fingers touched soft, warm curls.

Silas fell on his knees to examine this marvel. It was a sleeping child. A fair little thing with yellow curls all over its head. But how had it come in without him knowing? He stirred the fire and threw on dry sticks to brighten the flame. At this, the child awoke, and cried, 'Mammy!'

Silas lifted it up on to his knee and it flung its arms round his neck. As he held the child, he realized that its boots were wet. 'She's been walking in the snow!' he told himself, and hurried to the door. As soon as he opened it, the child cried, 'Mammy!' once more.

Bending and peering, Silas saw the row of tiny footprints that led to his cottage.

Still holding the child close, he followed the track to the lane and bushes, where he found Molly, lying dead and covered in snow.

The Squire's guests had fed well, drunk well and were relaxed and at their ease. The servants, now that supper was over, came to watch the dancing and to exclaim over the dress and behaviour of the dancers. It was before this great laughing chattering crowd that Silas made his appearance. A silence fell at once, and all eyes stared at him in astonishment.

'How's this?' asked the Squire, coming forward. 'What's this? What do you mean coming in here in this way – and with a child?'

'I've come for a doctor,' said Silas. 'I want the doctor. There's a woman lying in the snow, close by my cottage. She's dead, I think. The child must have been with her.'

Godfrey, who had come to the weaver's side, glanced at the child in Silas's arms. He saw at once, with a dreadful leap of his heart, that it was his own small daughter.

So Molly had carried out her threat, he thought. But was she dead, as Silas had said? If she were dead, then his troubles were all but over! In the next moment he was horrified by this ugly thought, for Godfrey Cass was at heart, a kind and gentle man.

The ladies of the party, having got over their surprise, were beginning to cluster round Silas and to ask whose child it was.

'Some poor woman found dead in the lane,' the Squire's housekeeper told them, bustling forwards and holding out her arms to take the child.

'Better leave it here, Master Marner,' she said.

Great was her surprise when Silas backed away from her, clasping the child more closely than ever.

'No!' he said. 'I can't part with it! It came to *me*.'

The ladies exclaimed in astonishment at this. Godfrey took matters into his own hands.

'I'll go for the doctor,' he said. 'I'll find the doctor. Go with Silas to his cottage and bring Dolly Winthrop to him, to help him.'

All agreed that this was by far the best course of action to be taken.

The woman had been laid in the cottage on the weaver's narrow bed. It was Molly. Godfrey saw that at once. She had been dead for some time the doctor said.

Godfrey, after one glance, turned to Silas who sat by the fire, the child still cradled in his arms. She was awake now and smiling up at the old weaver as if he were someone she had known and trusted all her short life.

'You'll take her to the parish workhouse tomorrow?' said Godfrey. He gazed at the child in Silas's arms and thought with a pang that she was, after all, his own daughter, his flesh and blood. But the workhouse was the place for her, he told himself. With the child out of sight he could perhaps begin to put the whole matter of his secret marriage out of his mind for ever.

'Who says?' asked Silas, sharply. 'Will they *make* me take her?'

'No,' said Godfrey, 'but surely an old man like yourself wouldn't want to keep a child?'

'She came to *me*,' Silas said again. 'Her mother's dead and, as far as anyone knows, she has no father. She's a lonely thing, like me. My money's gone, I don't know where – and now this has come, from I don't know where.'

It was plain that he did not mean to give up the child.

Godfrey felt in his pocket and brought out a golden guinea. 'Then let me give you something towards her keep,' he said.

He left the cottage and made his way back to the Red House. 'I'm free! I'm free!' he repeated to himself as he went. He could now ask Nancy Lammeter to marry him, for Molly would carry his secret to her grave!

Dunsey might come back, that was true, but his silence could always be bought.

CHAPTER 10

Silas and Eppie

The next day, when Dolly Winthrop came to the cottage, Silas showed her the money that Godfrey had given him.

'No need for new clothes!' said the practical Dolly. 'I've lots of clothes that Aaron wore when he was her age.'

She took the child on her knee and ran her fingers through the golden curls. 'An angel in heaven couldn't be more pretty!' she said. 'And I think that an angel was watching over her that night when her poor mother froze to death in the snow. It's like night and day, sunshine and shadow. One goes and the other comes.'

'Yes,' said Silas. 'My money went, and she came.'

'Well, she must be christened, Master Marner,' said Dolly.

'I shall call her Eppie,' said Silas. 'That was my mother's name, and the name of my little sister who died.'

So the child was christened Eppie, and as time went by Silas was reminded more and more of Dolly's words. 'Like night and day, shadow and sunshine. One goes, the other comes.' The sorrow had been lifted from his life, he thought, and his days were now filled with happiness.

He took Eppie with him wherever he went. Together they delivered the finished linen, and at every house and farmstead he was given ale, and Eppie had cakes and milk. He was asked a hundred times to retell the story of how she had wandered into his cottage, like a little robin seeking warmth from the cold. It was a tale that he liked, to tell.

Silas loved his foundling. He cherished and pampered her, could deny her nothing and, by the time she was three, Eppie was full of mischief! He had to watch her all the time and to stop her wandering was forced to tie her to his loom so that he might work with an easy mind. For this purpose he used a narrow strip of linen, long enough to let Eppie roam about the room and a little way outside.

He imagined that in doing this he had found the answer to his problem – and so he had until Eppie discovered his scissors and cut herself free.

When Silas looked up from his loom and saw that she was gone he was filled with fear. He ran in terror from the cottage, shouting her name. As he drew near to the Stone-pits his heart beat faster. Could Eppie have wandered to that awful place with its deep stretches of water, where the stone had been quarried? But Eppie was not there.

Silas turned and searched the lanes and fields, until at

last her found her, sitting by a little muddy pond and filling her shoes with water.

He carried her home, thinking about the advice that had been given to him by Dolly Winthrop.

'When she is naughty you must punish her, Master Marner,' she had said. 'A smack, that is what she needs.'

'Oh, I could never smack her!' said Silas.

'Then you must find another way, otherwise she will just go on being naughty. Why don't you do as I used to do with my Aaron when he was naughty – I used to lock him in the coal-hole. Not for long mind you, only for a minute or so, but it taught him a lesson! He didn't like that coal-hole one little bit!'

'Eppie must go into the coal-hole,' he said sadly, as he

carried the child home.

He expected tears when he closed the door on her, thought that she would sob and wail, but there was silence, until a little voice cried, 'Opy! Opy!'

Silas let her out. 'Now Eppie will never be naughty again,' he said. 'If she is, then she'll go back into that black place.'

Silas changed her clothes, for they were full of coal dust, and then went back to his work. He glanced at the linen band that he used to tie Eppie to the loom, and decided not to use it. He was sure that she had learned her lesson.

A few minutes later he looked up, and saw with a start that the room seemed empty. Then he saw her peeping at him from the 'black place'.

'Eppie in de tole-hole,' she said, with a cheeky smile.

That was the first and last time that Silas tried to punish Eppie. Smacks and coal-holes might do for the children of others, he thought, but he understood his Eppie, and knew the best way to treat her.

Everyone in Raveloe knew the child, and watched her grow; one watched her with special keenness – her father, Godfrey Cass. But he could do little for her without causing people to wonder why he took such an interest. In time he might, perhaps, be able to do more. In the meanwhile, he was happy just to know that she was cared for and loved.

Dunsey did not return, and Godfrey rode every day to visit Nancy Lammeter. She now found him to be a different man, and soon the date of their wedding was set.

PART TWO

CHAPTER 11

Eppie and Aaron

Sixteen years passed, and on a bright Sunday morning, three people were to be seen coming from church. They were Silas, now an elderly-looking man, although his age was no more than fifty-five, Eppie, a pretty eighteen-year-old, and Aaron. Aaron was a fine young man of twenty-four. It is clear to all who see them that he doted on Eppie.

The three walked together down the lanes, and Eppie admired the gardens.

'I wish that *we* could have a garden, Father,' said Eppie.

Before Silas could say that it might be possible, Aaron made his offer. 'I'll make you a garden, Eppie!' he said eagerly.

'Thank you, Aaron,' said Silas, 'but won't that make a lot of work for you?'

'Not at all!' said Aaron. 'Mr Godfrey will let me have some soil from his own garden, and as for plants, there are so many cuttings that folk throw away that Miss Eppie can have her garden in no time at all!'

'Well now. I reckon it's true what you say about the

cuttings,' said Silas. 'And that Mr Cass would let us have some good garden soil, but I don't want to be putting on good nature. He has done so much for us already. He built us an extra room on the cottage, he's given us furniture . . .'

'Mr Godfrey won't mind the soil,' said Aaron, cutting in on Silas's speech. 'Trust me, Master Marner.'

They reached the weaver's cottage and said goodbye to Aaron. Eppie laid the table for their meal, and after they had eaten she suggested that they take a walk together to the Stone-pits.

'Father,' Eppie said suddenly, as they strolled down the lane, 'if I married, could I use my mother's ring?'

The question shocked Silas. Eppie had known for a long time that he was not her real father, and that her mother had died in the snow close by the cottage. When she was fifteen Silas had given her the ring that had been taken from Molly's hand on the night she died. It had not been spoken of again until this moment.

'Why, Eppie,' he asked gently, 'are you thinking of marrying?'

'Aaron talked about it,' said Eppie.

'And what did he say?' asked Silas.

'Just that most folk get married, and that he would rather marry me than anyone else! But, father,' she went on, 'I wouldn't want to marry for a long time yet, and when I did, I should never leave you!'

They reached the Stone-pits and were surprised to find how low the water lay. 'New drains have been laid in the fields.' Silas told her. 'Soon the whole of Stone-pits will be as dry as a bone.'

That same evening, Nancy sat alone in the parlour of the Red House, for Godfrey had also gone to look at the new drains. She was turning the pages of the Bible, but was

not reading. Her thoughts had wandered instead to her life with Godfrey over the past fifteen years. They had been happy years, but for one thing – Nancy had borne no children. When she married she had expected to become a mother and looked forward to the time when her children would play about her feet. A drawer in her room was filled with tiny clothes that she had made for her first baby, a baby that was never born. Her sorrow because of her childless state was great, and grew as time went by.

Some years ago, Godfrey had suggested that they adopt a child, thinking that this would make Nancy happy. But Nancy thought that to adopt a child was to go against what God had planned for their lives.

'There is nothing at all wrong with adopting a child,' Godfrey said. 'Look at the girl in the weaver's cottage. Silas took her in and she has brought him nothing but happiness.'

'But he did not *seek* the child,' said Nancy. 'She came to *him*, like a gift from the Lord himself.'

Now, Nancy sat alone, thinking that perhaps she ought to have done as Godfrey said. Perhaps *he* minded their childless state as much as she did, but had said nothing. She wished that he were with her now, so that she might ask him.

Her maid, Jane, brought in a tray with tea things, and

Nancy turned to her.

'Is your master in yet, Jane?' she asked.

'No, ma'am, he isn't,' said Jane. 'I don't know if you noticed, ma'am, but there's folk making haste outside the front window, all going the same way. And there's not a man to be found in the yard.'

'Oh, I daresay that farmer Snell's bull has got loose again,' said Nancy.

'Then I hope that he won't gore anyone!' said Jane, leaving the room.

'That girl is always terrifying me!' thought Nancy. 'I *wish* that Godfrey would come!'

CHAPTER 12

The Discovery

Scarcely had Nancy made this wish, than the door opened and she saw that it was her husband. He was deathly white and trembling and she hurried to his side.

'Sit down, Nancy,' he said, taking her hands in his own. 'I came as quickly as I could, so that I could be the one to tell you the news.'

'Not my father, my sister . . .?' cried Nancy.

'No, it is news of no one living. It's of Dunsey, my brother Dunsey, whom we lost sight of sixteen years ago. Nancy, we've found him – found his body, his skeleton . . .'

He was silent for a moment and Nancy waited calmly for his next words.

'The Stone-pits have gone dry, due to the draining, and there he lies. There he's lain for sixteen years, wedged between two great stones. There's his watch, and there's my gold-handled hunting whip with my name on it that he took without my permission the day that he rode to the hunt on Wildfire.'

He paused once more, then carried on.

'And there's Silas's gold. Dunsey was the one who robbed Silas Marner. He must have lost his way after the theft and fallen into the Stone-pits.'

'Oh, Godfrey!' said Nancy. She was about to say more, but instinct told her that there was something else that Godfrey wished to tell her.

'Everything comes to light, Nancy,' he said at last. 'When God wills it, our secrets are found out.'

Nancy's feeling of dread returned, but she sat still and quiet and waited for him to go on.

'When I married you, Nancy, I hid something from you – something that I ought to have told you. The woman that Marner found dead in the snow was my wife – Eppie's mother. Eppie is my child.'

At his words, he felt Nancy take her hands from his.

'Nancy,' he said, his voice trembling, 'you will never think the same of me again.'

Nancy did not speak for some moments, then she turned to him, her eyes filled with tears.

'Oh, Godfrey!' she said. 'If you had told me this years ago, we could have taken her for our own. She would have loved me as a mother. Do you think that I would have refused her, knowing that she was yours?'

'But you wouldn't have married me!' cried Godfrey.

'I can't say *what* I would have done, Godfrey,' she replied. There was a faint sad smile about her mouth as she spoke these words.

'I am a worse man than you thought I was,' said Godfrey, 'but can you forgive me?'

'If you did wrong to me then you have made it up by your goodness to me these past fifteen years.' She told him. 'The greater wrong was to your wife and to Eppie.'

'But we can take her now!' cried Godfrey. 'I won't mind the world knowing at last!'

'It's not like taking in a tiny child,' said Nancy, 'but it's your duty to provide for her. And I will do my best for her, and hope that she will come to love me as a mother.'

'We'll go together to Silas's this very night,' said Godfrey, 'as soon as everything is quiet at the Stone-pits.'

CHAPTER 13

Godfrey's Wish

At eight that evening, Silas and Eppie were alone in the stone cottage. Eppie had drawn her chair close to Silas's and she sat holding his hands in hers. Between them, on the table lay the gold, lit by candlelight. Silas had stacked it into neat piles, just as he had done for so many years past. As he worked, he told Eppie of how he used to count it every night, how it had been his only joy in life.

'Until you came, my dear. At first I wished that you might turn back into gold, but that feeling did not last, so quickly did I become used to the sight of your pretty little face, the touch of your hand, the sound of your voice. You became my life, and now that . . .' he nodded towards the gleaming stacks on the table, 'that means nothing to me now. You can't know what your old father has felt for you.'

'But I do know father,' said Eppie,' and if it hadn't been for you, I would have been taken to the workhouse, where there would have been no love at all for me.'

At that moment there was a knocking at the door. Eppie rose to open it.

'Well, Silas,' said Godfrey, 'it's a great comfort to me to see you with your money again. It is a great grief to me to know that a member of my own family took it from you. But now I have come to make all that up to you, at least in some part.'

'Sir, I already have enough to thank you for,' said Silas. 'And as for the robbery, you couldn't help it. It was none of your doing.'

Godfrey and Nancy glanced at one another. They had agreed that the subject of Eppie's real father should be approached with care. The truth would come as a great shock to her.

'You may look at it in that way, Marner,' said Godfrey, 'but I never can. And I must act in a way that my own feelings tell me I must. Now, you have been a hard-working man all your life.' He paused and looked keenly at the old weaver.

'I have sir,' replied Silas, 'and that is what has kept me going.'

'But you are getting on in years, and that money on the table won't last forever. You've got two mouths to feed for a good many years to come.'

'Oh, I'm in no fear of want,' said Silas. 'Eppie and me will do well enough.'

'Silas,' said Godfrey, 'you have done everything that you could for Eppie for sixteen years. Would it not be a

great comfort to you to see her well provided for? She looks pretty and healthy enough, but not fit for any hardships. You'd like to see her taken care of by those who could make a lady of her? She's more fit for that than for a rough life, such as she might have in a few years' time.'

'I don't understand you, sir,' said Silas.

'I mean this, Marner,' said Godfrey. 'Mrs Cass and I have no children, as you know. We would like to adopt Eppie and bring her up as our own. Eppie, I am sure, will always love you and come to see you often.'

Eppie, who was standing behind Silas, felt his distress at these words. She reached out and put her hands on his shoulders, and felt him tremble. The words that Godfrey had spoken had seemed unreal to her, like words heard in a dream. Now she realized that he had spoken them in earnest. Before she could speak, Silas put his hand over her own.

'Eppie, my child,' he said, 'speak. I won't stand in your way if to become a lady is what you want.'

Eppie stepped forward at this. Her cheeks were flushed and her eyes bright with tears.

'Thank you, ma'am, sir,' she said, dropping a little curtsey, 'but I don't want to be a lady – thank you all the same.'

Her lips trembled as she spoke and she returned to stand by her father's chair and put her arms round his neck.

'I could have no happiness in life if I was away from Father. And I couldn't bear to think of him being here alone. Before he had me, he had no one. I had no one, too. He took care of me, and loved me, and I love him.'

'Are you sure now, Eppie?' said Silas. 'Are you sure you've made the right choice?'

'Yes, Father,' said Eppie. 'This is my home, this is where I belong.'

'But I have a claim on you, Eppie,' said Godfrey. 'The

strongest claim of all.'

He turned to Silas. 'It's my duty, Marner, to tell you that Eppie is my child. The woman you found dead in the snow all those years ago was my wife.'

Eppie gave a start at these words, and turned pale. Silas though remained calm; Eppie had declared that she would never leave him, and he knew this to be true.

'Then why did you not claim her sixteen years ago, sir?' he asked. 'God gave her to me because you turned your back on her. He looks upon her as mine, and you have no right to her.'

Godfrey remained silent at this, and after a swift

glance at her husband, Nancy spoke.

'It's only natural that you would want to stay here,' she said to Eppie, 'in the home that you know and with the father that you know. But I think that you have a duty to your lawful father. He has opened his home to you, and I don't think it right that you have turned your back on him.'

Eppie's eyes filled with tears at Nancy's words. 'I can't feel as I've got any father but one. I was brought up among poor folk, and can't turn my mind to becoming a lady.'

The tears fell and she brushed them away.

'I've promised to marry a working man, and he'll come to live here and help me care for Father. It's all I want.'

Godfrey rose, and turned to Nancy. 'Let's go,' he said quietly. Taking her arm, he walked out of cottage, unable to say another word.

CHAPTER 14

The Return to Lantern Yard

'Eppie, my dear,' said Silas, the next morning. 'There's something I've had on my mind to do for some time. Now that I have the money, I can do it. We'll ask Dolly to look after the house, and we'll pack a few things and set out.'

'To where, Father?' asked Eppie.

'To the town where I was born and lived for many years – to Lantern Yard. I want to see Mr Paston, the minister. Something may have come up during the past years that would prove my innocence of the robbery.'

Eppie was excited at the thought of visiting a big town, and Dolly Winthrop was pleased at the thought that Silas might be able, at last, to clear his name. 'You'll be easier in your mind for the rest of your life, Master Marner,' she said.

So, a few days later, Silas and Eppie set out, wearing their Sunday clothes and with a small bundle tied in a blue linen cloth.

The change in Lantern Yard bewildered Silas. There seemed nothing left that he recognized until they came Prison Street.

'There's the jail, Eppie,' he said. 'I know my way now. It's the third turning on the left.'

But when they turned, Silas stopped in amazement. A large factory stood before them, from which men and women were streaming for their midday meal.

'It's gone, Eppie,' he said, when he could speak. 'All of it gone – the chapel, the houses, the weaving shed.'

'Come, Father,' said Eppie. 'Let's go into that little brush shop over there. Perhaps they may be able to tell us something.'

But the owner of the brush shop knew nothing about Lantern Yard, nor did anyone else in the street.

'The old place has been swept away,' Silas told Dolly, on their return to the cottage. 'I shall never know if anyone found out the truth about the robbery. I shall put it clear from my mind, and think of it no more.'

CHAPTER 15

A Wedding

Eppie and Aaron were married in the spring, when the gardens of Raveloe were full of lilac and laburnum. Her wedding dress was one that Nancy Cass had bought for her, and the wedding feast, which was held at the Rainbow Inn, was paid for by Godfrey Cass.

After the service, Eppie came from the church with Aaron on one arm and Silas on the other. The three strolled through the village, and paused where Mr Macey sat by his front door. He was too old to attend the wedding, and very glad to be able to speak to them.

'Well, Master Marner,' he said. 'I've lived to see my words come true! I was the first to say that there was no harm in you. And the first to say that your gold would come back to you. And I was right on both counts.'

Eppie had a larger garden than she ever expected. The house too had been enlarged, at the expense of Godfrey Cass, to suit Silas's larger family. Both he and Eppie had declared that they would rather stay at the stone cottage than move to another home.

The garden was fenced with stones on two sides, but in front there was an open fence through which bright flowers peeped as if in welcome.

'Oh, Father!' said Eppie. 'What a lovely home ours is! I don't think anybody could be happier than we are.'